Hello, Reader!

MEET TIBBAR JACK.

He's the WRONG-WAY RABBIT!
He walks backwards.
He talks backwards.
And he is very funny.

You will like this silly story!

For Ykceb and Alil Seilugram — T.S.

Library of Congress Cataloging-in-Publication Data

Slater, Teddy.
    The Wrong-Way Rabbit / by Teddy Slater: illustrated by Diane de Groat.
     p.   cm. — (Hello reader)
    Summary: Tibbar the backward bunny does everything the opposite
from what's expected, walking backwards and going up the down stairs.

    [1. Rabbits — Fiction. 2. Individuality — Fiction. 3. Stories in rhyme.]
I. de Groat, Diane, ill. II. Title. III. Series.
PZ8.3.S6318Bac   1993
[F] — dc20   92-14334
                                              CIP
                                              AC

ISBN 0-590-90762-X

28 27 26 25 24   16/0

Printed in the U.S.A.   40

First Scholastic printing, February 1993

The WRONG-WAY RABBIT

by Teddy Slater
Illustrated by Diane de Groat

Hello Reader!—Level 2

SCHOLASTIC INC.
New York London Toronto Auckland Sydney

Chapter 1
HERE COMES TIBBAR JACK

Hippity-hop,
it's Tibbar Jack,
a very mixed-up bunny.

The way he talks is funny.

"Good night!" he sings out every day,
just as the sun comes up.

He pours his juice into his bowl,
his cornflakes in his cup.

Jack wears his sweater inside out.

His socks go on his ears.
Of course, he can't
hear much that way. . . .

It drives his mom to tears.

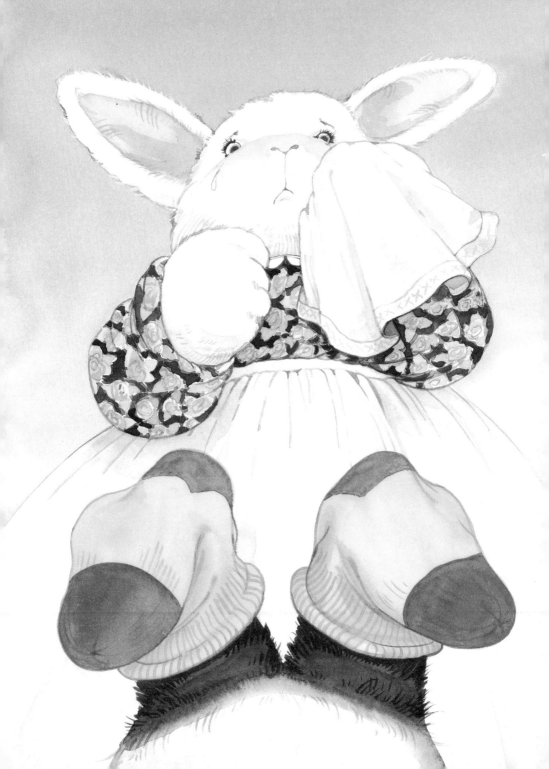

"Go to town and buy some oats,"
his mother said one day.

But Tibbar did not hear her right. . . .

What else is there to say?

Chapter 2
T. J. GOES TO SCHOOL

Tickity-tock!
It's eight o'clock —
time to go to school.

Sometimes Jack acts silly,
but this bunny is no fool.

T.J. knows his CBA's.

Hear him count to ten:
"Thirteen, twelve, eleven, ten . . ."

20 19 18 17 16

and then he starts again.

15   14   13   12   11   10

15   14

In the **OUT** door Tibbar goes . . .

up the stairs marked **DOWN**.

He always paints his cows bright blue.
He makes his skies light brown.

When everybody cuts and pastes,
Tibbar pastes and cuts.

He likes to do things his own way.
It drives his teacher nuts.

Chapter 3
GOOD NIGHT, TIBBAR JACK

Rub-a-dub-dub
and into the tub,
Jack steps with all his clothes.

When he is wet,
he gets undressed.
That's how his bath time goes.

At seven-thirty on the dot,
Mom tucks her son in bed.

But Tibbar never sleeps at night.
He'd rather play instead.

Jack likes his story back to front,
the end before the start.
That way he knows how things turn out.
It makes him feel quite smart.

Inside out and upside down,
Jack's always looking back.
Things sure can get confusing
when your name is Tibbar Jack.

Yes, living life the way Jack does
is more than just a habit.
And if you haven't guessed it yet . . .

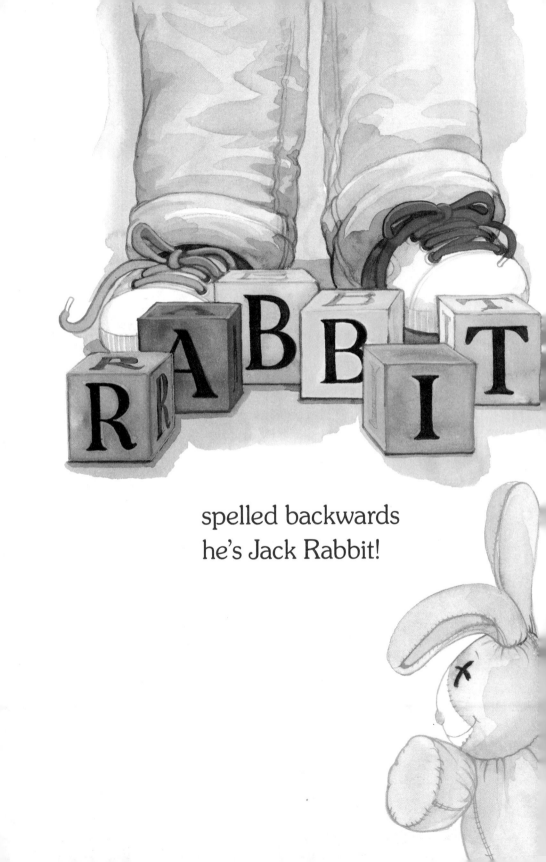

spelled backwards
he's Jack Rabbit!